YOU CAN'T CUDDLE A CROCODILE

For Freya,
with love from Granny
D.H.

For Theodore and Nancy,
my little monkeys! xx
E.E.

First published in 2019 by Hodder Children's Books

Hodder Children's Books
An imprint of Hachette Children's Group
Part of Hodder & Stoughton
Carmelite House, 50 Victoria Embankment
London, EC4Y 0DZ

A catalogue record of this book is available from the British Library.

HB ISBN: 978 1 444 92454 1
PB ISBN: 978 1 444 92455 8

1 3 5 7 9 10 8 6 4 2
Printed in China

An Hachette UK Company
www.hachette.co.uk
www.hachettechildrens.co.uk

Hodder
Children's
Books

YOU CAN'T CUDDLE A CROCODILE

Diana Hendry

Illustrated by Ed Eaves

On Monday
my sister's a monkey.

"I wonder what monkeys eat for breakfast?" asks Mum.

"It's not easy eating
anything when you're
upside
down!"
says Dad.
JABBER!
JABBER!
JABBER!

"I think Monkey's saying something," says Mum. "Only I don't understand monkey language."

"It's **bananas!"** I shout.

"So it is," says Mum. "Silly me."

FLAKE

On Tuesday my sister's a bear.

"Please, no more hugs!" says Mum.
"I need to do the washing up."

"Whoops!"

says Dad. "I think I've just tripped over a sulky bear."

GRRRRR!

“Has anyone seen the cat?” asks Mum.

“We’re hiding from the bear,” I whisper.

EEEEEK!

On Wednesday
Mum takes us to the beach.

My sister's a camel.

Over the desert we go.

"Where's my rug gone?" calls Mum.

On Thursday we go shopping in the rain.

"Is there something the matter with your sister?" asks the shopkeeper. "She's got very odd feet."

"I don't have a sister," I say . . .

“I’ve got a penguin!”

Shopping takes a long time
when you have flippers.

But sliding is faster.

WHEEEEE!
FLIP FLAP!
FLIP FLAP!

On Friday
Dad reads us a bedtime story.
My sister's a crocodile.

"Oh dear," says Dad. "I do miss my little girl.

You can't **cuddle** a crocodile."

"Do you think crocodiles like stories?" asks Mum.

"Yes, if they're snappy!" Dad and I say together.

SNIP
SNAP!
SNIP
SNAP!
SNIP
SNAP!

On Saturday my sister's a lion.
She goes prowling about the garden, roaring.

The postman looks very scared.

"It's all right," I tell him.
"It's only my sister.
My sister's a ZOO!"

“I liked it better when she was your sister,” the postman says.

“So did I,” I say.

But on Sunday . . .

. . . my sister's my sister again.

She's Freya all day long.

"Oh!" says Mum.
"You're back!
Welcome home.
Where's your brother?"

"He's up in the garden,"
says my sister.

I'm a giraffe!

Who's got the

last laugh?